For Brian Williams. J.W.

Also by Jeanne Willis and Tony Ross:

Flabby Cat and Slobby Dog

Fly, Chick, Fly!

Hippospotamus

American edition published in 2014 by Andersen Press USA, an imprint of Andersen Press Ltd.

www.andersenpressusa.com

First published in Great Britain in 2014 by Andersen Press Ltd., 20 Vauxhall Bridge Road, London SW1V 2SA.

Published in Australia by Random House Australia Pty., Level 3, 100 Pacific Highway, North Sydney, NSW 2060.

Distributed in the United States and Canada by

Lerner Publishing Group, Inc.

241 First Avenue North

Minneapolis, MN 55401 USA

For reading levels and more information, look up this title at www.lernerbooks.com.

Color separated in Switzerland by Photolitho AG, Zürich.

Printed and bound in Malaysia by Tien Wah Press.

Tony Ross has used pen, ink and watercolor in this book.

Library of Congress Cataloging-in-Publication data available.

ISBN: 978-1-4677-3450-9

eBook ISBN: 978-1-4677-3455-4

1 - TWP - 10/31/13

FSC
www.fsc.org
MIX
Paper from
responsible sources
FSC® C012700

Jeanne Willis

Tony Ross

BOA'S BAD BIRTHDAY

ANDERSEN PRESS USA

It was Boa's birthday.
It was going to be the best one ever.
Or so he hoped.

He invited his friends.
They would all bring him wonderful presents.
Or would they?

Orangutan's was enormous.
"Please don't let it be
what I think it is,"
thought Boa.
But it was . . .

. . . a piano!

Boa couldn't play it. He had no fingers.
"It's the thought that counts," said his mother.

Orangutan clearly hadn't thought very hard,
but maybe Monkey had. He was clever.
Or was he?

His parcel looked **very** interesting . . .

. . . sunglasses!

"Everyone's wearing them," said Monkey.
But Boa wasn't. They kept slipping off.
He had no ears or nose.
"Thanks," said Boa. "They're lovely."

But, secretly, he was deeply disappointed.
"Third time lucky," said his mother.

Jaguar arrived with a neat package.
"I hope you like them!" he said.

Boa hoped so too.
He could hardly wait to unwrap it.

"I thought they'd be useful," said Jaguar.
But they weren't. They were . . .

. . . mittens!

"Do you like the color?" asked Jaguar.
"It's my favorite," said Boa.

But what he really wanted to say was,
"Why buy me mittens? Are you crazy?

I have no hands!"

But that would have been rude.
It was kind of his friends
to get him anything.
Perhaps Sloth's gift would
be more suitable.

But it wasn't. It was a . . .

. . . hairbrush!

"It's a very good one," insisted Sloth.

But it was no good for Boa.

He had no hair!

"Open my parcel," said Ant Eater.
"You'll have great fun with it!"

But Boa didn't.
It was a . . .

. . . soccer ball!

It was no fun at all!
Boa couldn't kick it.
He had no feet!

It was Boa's worst birthday ever.

All his gifts were rubbish.

And just when he thought things
couldn't get any worse . . .

"Dung Beetle's here!" said his mother.
"I bet her present is a pile of
You Know What," thought Boa.

And he was right!

But he was also wrong,
because in the dung ball, there was a seed.
And when it rained, it sprouted.

And it grew …

And it grew …

And it grew into …

...a beautiful tree!

It was the perfect present for a boa.
It was the right size. The right shape . . .

. . . and it suited Boa down to the ground.
It was just what he had always wanted.

So if you ever get a present that stinks, say thank you.
Because it might turn out to be . . .

...the **best** present **ever!**